George Frideric Handel

For my wife, Elizabeth,
and 25 years of brilliant harmonies and spirited counterpoint.
—D.C.

For my best friend, my wife Amanda.
I did not understand worship until I met you!
—J.W.

This book was designed in QuarkXPress, with type set in 16 point Galliard.

The artist would like to give a special thank you to all of the following people:
John Carvalho of Exposures Photography for being the best Handel in town.
Michael Driedger as Thomas, Manny Fantridakis, Kevin Fuhro, Lori Olejnik, Stan Olthuis.
Yüksel Hassan, thank you for your endless patience with such a meandering project.
Amanda Grant, my beautiful wife. Brenden Crookshank, the best hockey player in Mt. Bridges.
Clarissa Morawski, Maija-Liisa Harju, Chris Lavis, Maciek Szczerbowski, Theatrix Costume.
A very special thanks to the CBC Wig and Costume departments.

National Library of Canada Cataloguing in Publication

Cowling, Douglas
Hallelujah Handel / Douglas Cowling ; illustrated by Jason Walker.

Based on musical drama for children.
ISBN 0-7791-1391-8

1. Handel, George Frideric, 1685-1759—Juvenile fiction.
I. Walker, Jason II. Title.

PS8555.O887H33 2002   jC813'.6   C2002-901631-2 PZ7

6 5 4 3 2 1   Printed and bound in Canada   02 03 04 05

Hallelujah Handel

text by

Douglas Cowling

art by

Jason Walker

North Winds Press

A Division of Scholastic Canada Ltd.

"The King is coming!" A voice rang out over the excited crowd. Thomas and his friends pushed forward to the edge of the dock. Everyone wanted to catch a glimpse of the royal barge. Elegant ladies in rustling silks jostled with scruffy beggars on the narrow embankment. Cannons fired and trumpets blazed as the fleet of golden boats glided across the waters.

Thomas had never seen the King before. And now he could almost stretch out his hand and touch him.

Harry poked Thomas in the ribs. "The King is smiling!"

A murmur went through the crowd. The King never smiled. But there he was, a great grin on his face as he came ashore.

"Mr. Handel's Water Music has tickled him," someone called out, and even the soldiers of the guard caught themselves laughing.

Thomas heard the musicians' boat bump the dock with a thud. He turned to see George Frideric Handel stand up and wave to the applauding onlookers. There he was . . . a real composer. For a moment Thomas thought he could hear music. But it was only the cry of the seabirds overhead.

"Quick, lads," Jack whispered, as he scrambled toward the boat. "I see a penny's work for us!"

$\mathcal{M}$aster Handel, too, had a smile on his face. The musicians had played his music for the King's journey. Up the river, down the river, and all through dinner. And now he could feel the King's gold coins jangling in his pocket.

Harry jumped onto the gangplank and took off his tattered hat.

"A penny to carry your instruments, Sir?" he pleaded. "Jack and Thomas, they be good boys for the work, too."

The three ragged street boys looked up hopefully as Handel came down the gangplank. Thomas stared at the mountainous figure with the wig like a storm cloud.

Handel eyed the boys from under his grey curls. How did they live, alone on the streets?

"Can you carry my harpsichord without dropping it into the water?" he growled playfully.

"Yes, Sir," Jack said, and pushed Thomas forward. "We know all about things musical. Thomas here can sing wonderful fine."

Harry leaned close to Handel and whispered to him, "He can't speak, truth be told. But we look after him."

Handel looked closely at Thomas. "A silent angel — how sad. What made you stop speaking?"

Thomas turned away quickly. Harry and Jack had already jumped over the railing and were struggling to carry the harpsichord onto the dock. Thomas held the carriage door open.

Handel fished in his pocket. "Well done, good fellows all," he said.

The boys doffed their caps as Handel counted out their pennies.

"Home to Brook Street, my good man!" he shouted to the driver. As the carriage pulled away, Thomas wanted to call out, to bring him back. But no sound came out.

*S*uddenly a hand gripped Thomas's shoulder and spun him around roughly. It was the Keeper. Everything the boys earned, begged, and sometimes stole went to the cruel and greedy Keeper. The boys hated him. But without the Keeper, where would they find food or a safe place to sleep?

"Give me the money, boy," the Keeper demanded.

Thomas dropped his coins into the Keeper's hand. His dirty fingers closed quickly around them.

"That ain't enough," the man growled, and raised his fist angrily. The boys caught his arm.

"Thomas will sing tonight, Keeper," Jack promised. "He'll make you money. You know the ladies love his voice."

The Keeper looked at Thomas's frightened face. Then he laughed and spat on the ground.

"Get his singing clothes," he said. "We've got work to do."

Thomas was too tired to care where the Keeper was taking him that night. Jack and Harry had been left behind, locked up in the dismal room they called home. The streets were dark and cold. Thomas shivered as the Keeper pushed him along, always in the shadows. Just when the boy thought he could go no further, the Keeper knocked at a great oak gate. The door swung open. Thomas blinked in wonder.

Through the door, Thomas could see the ballroom of a great nobleman's palace. Mirrored candles and chandeliers sent glittering light over the guests: noble lords with glinting swords and fair ladies with diamonds flashing in their curls. The Keeper was haggling over money with a chamberlain.

"Threepence to hear the boy who sings like an angel," he demanded.

*T*homas moved forward, peeking around a pillar. His ears filled with the sweet sounds of flutes and violins. The dancers moved like marionettes, stiff and expressionless in their jewelled silks and powdered white wigs.

On a table, amidst all the flowers and silver plates, stood a little girl. Thomas was amazed at how still she stood. A living statue, a human centrepiece for the party.

She smiled at him shyly. "Have you come to sing?" she whispered.

Thomas nodded and backed away. He was afraid the Keeper would catch them talking.

The little girl's smile faded as a glittering, giggling lady swept into the room, loudly demanding a poem. The girl curtsied, then began to recite — a charming doll amusing the bored, wealthy guests.

Suddenly the orchestra began to play his song. The violins swelled in a sad melody, like unhappy tears dropping on the marble floor.

Thomas quickly slipped through the guests to the stage. All heads in the room turned to look at him. He shut his eyes against them and let the music fill his ears and his soul. The hunger and exhaustion of begging every day seemed to slip away.

He began to sing. The chattering of the guests stopped as the sound caught at their hearts.

"Give me my freedom from this cruel silence. Heavens, O grant me my liberty."

The music seemed to waver out of tune. Thomas gasped for breath. The candles began to swim before his eyes. What was happening?

*T*homas fell forward in a faint. Strong arms caught him.

"What is wrong, boy? Are you ill?" a deep voice asked.

Thomas opened his eyes. He was looking into the face of Master Handel. The composer held Thomas's trembling body in a safe embrace.

"You seem to have dropped from heaven," the composer smiled. "Where did you learn to sing my music?"

Thomas could only shake his head and close his eyes.

In a moment, the Keeper appeared beside Handel. He shifted from foot to foot in a nervous little dance.

"Master Handel, you must excuse me. The boy is a lazy scoundrel. He'll be punished for this, I promise you."

Handel looked closely at the Keeper without answering.

The Keeper continued, in an oily voice. "He sings his music right well, Sir, but he needs a firm hand. Yes, a firm hand, Sir."

Handel helped Thomas to his feet, but kept his hand on the boy's shoulder.

"He needs bread and milk, man, not a beating," he said. "Here, take this and see that he gets some food."

The Keeper bowed and took the coin. Handel turned to Thomas and smiled warmly.

"When you are better, come see me at the opera house. I will hear you sing again. Good night, my mysterious little friend."

Thomas watched Handel disappear into the crowd. He felt the Keeper's fingers on his arm like claws. He opened his mouth to cry for help. But nothing came out.

The Keeper hissed, "You'll regret this little charade tonight, my boy. Get going."

The lamplighter was making his way along the darkened street. Handel climbed into his carriage. From the shadows, he watched the Keeper and Thomas disappear down the narrow lane.

He rubbed his eyes. How weak his sight was becoming.

It began to rain.

Handel pulled his cloak around him, grumbling. "Rain, rain, rain," he complained. "How do these English stand it?"

Water drops streaked down the glass. Handel's thoughts returned to Thomas and his poor friends in the streets. Many years before, the composer had helped to raise money for the first orphanage in London. How proud he and his friends were of the new building. Finally, here was a place where lonely children would be safe. Safe from the streets where they lived in fear and misery.

But it wasn't enough.

What else could Handel do for the orphans that would open the hearts — and the purses — of all the people of London? Once again he heard Thomas's voice in his head. The melody floated up and was lost in the wind outside the carriage.

But it left behind the beginning of an idea. Tomorrow Handel would search out Thomas and his friends.

"*J*ack, Jack!" Harry shouted as he ran through the crowded market.

Jack was juggling oranges he had pinched from the fruit-seller's stall. Harry's voice made him drop the fruit. The crowd laughed as he scrambled to pick them up.

"What's wrong?" Jack asked. He had never seen Harry so frightened.

"He's gone!" Harry blurted out. "I can't find him anywhere!"

"Who? Thomas?" Jack asked, knowing the answer already.

"I've looked everywhere," Harry said desperately. "If the Keeper finds out . . ."

"We'll just have to find him first," Jack said grimly. The last time Thomas had disappeared, the Keeper had sworn that if it happened again, Jack and Harry would get a beating they would never forget.

Jack thought hard. The flash of an idea crossed his face.

"Why don't we see if Master Handel can help. Maybe Thomas tried to go visit him," he said.

Harry agreed. "I heard that he conducts his music along the promenade at Vauxhall Gardens. I'll bet that's where we'll find Master Handel."

The boys set off at a run.

George Frideric Handel was enjoying his walk in the park. Garlanded pavilions offered sweets and ices for every taste. In the trees above hung hundreds of tiny lanterns, like stars in the night sky. From every branch could be heard the happy songs of exotic birds in gilded cages. It was a magical fairyland.

Handel was now a famous man in London. He raised his hat and bowed as people recognized him and called out "Bravo!"

At one of the pavilions, an orchestra played. Handel sat down at a table. Immediately, the conductor stopped the music. The musicians craned their necks to catch a glimpse of the composer.

"Master Handel," the conductor asked, "What shall we play for you?"

Handel chuckled. "No more Water Music, I pray you, good sirs. My shoes are still wet from the last voyage."

The spectators laughed.

"Perhaps you can dry them out with a few fireworks!"

The crowd applauded and in a moment the orchestra blazed into sound with Handel's Music for the Royal Fireworks. The trumpets sounded, bright as lightning, while the drums shook the crystal lanterns with their thunder.

*H*andel stretched his legs, then jumped up in alarm. Someone was under his table!

"Come out this instant!" he said, raising his walking stick.

"It's only us, Jack and Harry," a voice said from under the table.

Handel lowered his stick as the two boys crawled out. "What are you two doing under there? And where is your little singing friend?" Handel asked.

"Master Handel, we need your help!" Harry's voice was filled with fear.

"Thomas has run away! We have to find him before the Keeper does!" Jack added.

Handel looked at the two frightened faces, covered with the dirt and grease of the streets.

"Quickly, come with me," he said.

Together they ran across the lawn to Handel's carriage and climbed into the soft, velvet-covered seats.

"Where do you think he went?" Handel asked.

The boys looked at each other and shrugged their shoulders helplessly.

"Maybe he went back to the orphanage," Harry suggested. "I heard he came from there, once."

Handel jumped at the idea. "We'll go there now," he said.

$\mathcal{H}$arry and Jack hardly knew what to expect. They had never gone beyond the alleys and back lanes of the Keeper's world. Now they were riding through the stone arches of the Foundling Hospital, the bright new school for orphans.

All around them girls and boys were at their lessons. On one bench, a group of girls sat practising their sewing, hoping to become seamstresses' apprentices or ladies' maids. A few older boys were braiding rope. In a few months, they might join the Royal Navy as cabin boys.

When the children saw Handel's carriage rattle into the courtyard, they dropped their work and ran over to greet him.

"A song for the master!" someone cried out.

The whole courtyard rang with the sound of children's voices: "See, the conquering hero comes, Sound the trumpets, beat the drums."

Handel clapped. "Well done. Such lovely music, too. Who composed it?" he asked mischievously.

"That was *your* music, Master Handel!" a little girl answered. Handel laughed.

"What music are you going to perform at our concert tomorrow?" an older boy asked.

"Ah, something very special — my Messiah. Will you all come?"

The children cheered.

"Children, children! Such a commotion! Back to your lessons," a voice called out behind them. A jovial matron strode toward them. Handel tipped his hat to her.

"My good woman," he asked, "do you know whether a boy named Thomas was ever a student at this school? You are sure to remember him. He cannot speak, but sings like an angel."

"Thomas! I could never forget Thomas," the woman replied. "Such a sweet lad. It's a pity he couldn't stay." She looked around and lowered her voice. "Some doctors examined him and decided he had an imbalance in his mind. They took him to be locked up, for his own safety, they said."

"Locked up!" Jack cried out. "Where?"

"He's never done anything wrong!" Harry said angrily.

The matron looked at the boys with sympathy, but shrugged her shoulders.

"I think we must visit Bedlam," Handel said softly.

The matron wiped away a tear with her apron. "Well, all I can say is, God bless him, if he's in that place."

"The madhouse," Jack whispered to himself, fear in his eyes.

Handel's carriage clattered through the crowded city. It was a maze of narrow streets and dark courtyards. Thieves and cut-throats waited in the shadows. There were no bright lights, no beautiful music; only the desperation of people trying to survive. Children often grew up alone here. When someone like the Keeper promised food and a place to sleep, children quickly fell under his control.

Jack and Harry sat well back from the windows.

"No use letting the Keeper know where we are," whispered Harry.

Handel said nothing. He wondered if the Keeper was out there, watching them, following them — perhaps ahead of them, closer than they were to finding Thomas. They had to find him first. But where?

Handel looked at the faces of Jack and Harry. Once again, he seemed to hear Thomas's voice rising above the clamour of the streets: "Come unto Him, all ye that labour, and He will give you rest."

It was the music of his Messiah. The voice faded in the tolling of a great bell. They had arrived at an ancient building with high stone walls and dark, covered windows.

"I don't like the look of this," Jack whispered.

*H*andel knocked on the heavy iron door. It opened, and in another moment they were inside the forbidding fortress.

"Stay close to me, boys," Handel said softly. "The Hospital of St. Mary of Bethlehem is a strange and disturbing place."

They walked silently down a long, dark corridor. Their footsteps echoed in the shadows. Through the open door at the end, they could see a doctor. Beside him, a boy sat in a chair with his head bowed. The doctor had a violin, and as he played, the boy shook his head slowly in time to the music.

"Is that Thomas?" Jack asked eagerly. The child turned at the sound.

"No, I'm afraid your friend is not here," the doctor replied. "This lad suffers terrible nightmares. My violin helps him sleep."

Jack and Harry watched as the child stood, then left the room without a word.

"But Thomas was here, wasn't he?" Handel asked. He tried not to let the boys hear the fear in his voice.

The doctor put down his violin and looked at them. His eyes were tired.

"I see so many unhappy people here, so many people with such dark secrets," he said. "But Thomas gave me hope."

"What happened?" Jack asked.

The doctor sighed. "A man came one day and offered to give Thomas a job singing in some sort of musical show. We had to let him go."

"Has he ever been back?" Jack asked.

"No one ever comes back to Bedlam, my boy," the doctor said softly. "I miss him. He was particularly fond of the songs of your Master Handel here. I marvelled at how many he knew, and how well he knew them."

Handel clapped his hands in excitement. "Of course, of course! That is the solution to our mystery!" he crowed. The boys looked at him in astonishment.

"Thank you, Doctor," Handel said. "Come, boys, we have not a minute to waste! We must go to find the place where Thomas learned my songs."

*T*he carriage rattled and jangled as the horses raced through the city. The boys pressed their faces against the windows, hoping to catch a glimpse of their friend. Finally, the carriage clattered to a stop before a huge door plastered with a poster:

OPERA
tonight by
Mr. Handel
SOLD OUT

"Why do you think he's hiding here?" Harry asked.

But Handel jumped out of the carriage and ran up the steps as quickly as his eyesight would allow. The boys raced to catch up with him.

"Hurry," Handel panted. "We must get inside before anyone recognizes me."

They climbed to the balcony of the theatre. They could hear the sounds of the orchestra tuning, and the boys peeked out from behind the box's red velvet curtains.

Jack and Harry could not believe their eyes. The stage shimmered in the light of candles hidden in the scenery. As the orchestra began to play, a painted cloud opened, and a beautiful queen floating down to the stage. It seemed as if she was singing to them alone.

"I love you, beloved, your eyes shine like starlight."

Handel's head turned in surprise.

"Listen!" he whispered. "There are two voices singing!"

"My heart feels your heart's fire. My heart burns for you."

The boys leaned forward. Yes, there was another voice, but far away, almost in another world.

"We must find that voice," Handel said firmly.

$\mathcal{H}$andel and the boys waited until the performance had finished. The audience applauded wildly and called out, "Bravo!" Jack and Henry grinned and pretended to bow behind the curtain. Slowly the crowd filed out. The theatre was silent and empty.

Handel took a lantern.

"Let us begin our search," he said.

Carefully they descended a creaking staircase. Their footsteps echoed in the looming darkness.

"Where are we? I don't like this much," Harry whispered.

Gradually their eyes began to pick out shapes in the darkness.

"This looks like a ship," said Harry.

"And over here; it's the queen's throne," Jack called out.

"We're backstage now," Handel replied. "These are the sets for my operas."

"Look out! It's a sea serpent," Jack shouted as he pushed a gigantic dragon toward them. In the flickering light, it almost looked real. Harry laughed.

"Quiet — I hear something," Handel whispered.

They stopped and listened. The shadows danced all around them.

"Someone's singing," Harry said. "It's coming from the stage."

They moved quietly toward the voice.

"Thomas!" Jack cried out.

Handel and the boys looked across the vast, empty stage. A single candle spread a pool of light in the darkness. Thomas knelt there alone, singing. His voice was filled with longing.

"I shall weep, alone in silence. Hear my sorrow and feel my sadness."

Handel came forward and gently touched the boy's shoulder.

"Ah, Thomas, you sing my music like a lost, lonely angel. You learned it here in the opera house, didn't you? Here in the darkness where you hid, first from the danger of the streets, then from the Keeper. Every night you heard the singers' voices rising clear and beautiful. They created a world for you that was safe and loving."

*T*homas lowered his head.

"The music found me once, too, Thomas," Handel continued.

Thomas looked up at him, surprised and curious.

"I too had a terrible shadow fall across my mind. I sat at the harpsichord, yet my fingers refused to play. But the music came and found me, like your song here tonight. It brought me back to the light, Thomas. And you will come back to us soon. I know it. I have a gift for you all."

"A gift? For us?" Harry asked.

Handel smiled. "And Thomas will unwrap it for everyone."

For a moment, Thomas hesitated. Then he smiled and held out his hand. Handel scooped him up in his arms and hugged him tight.

"Come on," Jack said excitedly. "I want to see Master Handel's gift!"

The sun was dawning over the steeples and domes of the city as they came out of the darkness of the opera house. The gentle canter of the horses soon lulled the boys to sleep. Handel smiled at the pile of dozing innocence.

The carriage stopped outside the gates of the orphanage.

Suddenly, a hand reached in through the open window. "His voice belongs to me. *I* own the little rat!"

The door opened and the Keeper jumped onto the carriage steps.

"This is the final chorus, Master Handel, and it ain't your song," he snarled.

Handel pushed the Keeper away and raised his walking stick. "You've lost them," Handel said firmly. "They belong here now. The music will keep them safe."

The Keeper paused and then spat at Handel's feet. "Take 'em if you will," he shouted. "There are more like them to be had in every street in London."

Handel lowered his cane and breathed heavily as the Keeper slipped into the darkness.

"Where are we? Are we almost there?" Jack mumbled. The boys yawned and stretched like cats in the morning light.

Handel began to sing,

"Arise, shine, for thy light is come!"

His deep bass voice boomed across the courtyard. Still singing, he strode toward the chapel where the orchestra could be heard tuning for rehearsal. Jack and Harry cheered and ran after him. Even Thomas broke into a run to catch them.

Sunlight poured through the tall windows of the chapel. The schoolchildren entered in pairs, each girl and boy holding hands. The orphans tried not to turn around and gawk at the musicians in the gallery. Handel took his seat at the keyboard, while Jack and Harry began to pump the bellows of the great organ. Thomas stood beside the organ with the singers.

The notes seemed to climb higher and higher, almost into heaven itself. The violins fluttered like angel wings. Handel raised his hand and Thomas began to sing.

"Fear not; for behold, I bring you good tidings of great joy."

The choir answered him, "Peace on earth!"

"Yes, Thomas," Handel whispered. "Peace on earth. Peace for you and for us all."

He lifted the music from the organ and gave it to Thomas. "This is my gift to you, and to the Foundlings. Whenever my Messiah is sung, people will open their hearts to remember children everywhere."

Thomas hesitated. Then his eyes filled with tears. He reached out for Master Handel's hand.

"I'm home," Thomas said.

His voice steadied.

"I'm home."

The candles in the chapel burned ever brighter, and the very angels of heaven seemed to sing for joy.

"Hallelujah!"

George Frideric Handel